Marigold did not agree with
her mother, or her father,
or her friend Maxine.
But she agreed with herself,
and that was the important thing.

THE ONE AND ONLY MARIGOLD

written by
FLORENCE
PARRY HEIDE

illustrated by
JILL
McELMURRY

 schwartz & wade books · new york

MARIGOLD'S NEW COAT

Marigold liked her old coat so much that she wore it all the time. She wore it outside, inside, and when she went to bed.

One day her mother said,
"Marigold, you need a new coat."
"I like this one," said Marigold.
"It's worn out," said her mother.
"I know," said Marigold. "That's why I like it."
"We're going to the store to buy you a new one,"
said Marigold's mother.
"I'm not going," said Marigold.
"And then we'll get a chocolate sundae with
whipped cream," said her mother.

"All right," said Marigold. "But I'm keeping my old coat, too. I'm a very loyal person."

At the store, there were many coats on the racks.

"This one is pretty," said Marigold's mother.

"It's ugly," said Marigold. "Green makes me look sick. Green makes me feel sick. If I have to wear it, I'll throw up."

"Here's a pretty coat," said the saleslady.

"It makes me look like a teddy bear," said Marigold. "If I wanted to look like a teddy bear, I'd get this coat."

"Here's a nice coat," said Marigold's mother.

"It's plaid," said Marigold. "I hate plaid. And I hate red and I hate green and I really hate red and green together. I look like a stoplight."

Marigold tried on striped coats

and checked ones,

plain coats

and fancy coats.

But there was no coat Marigold liked . . . until . . .

"This one!" said Marigold.

"I like this one!"

"I'm afraid we don't have that coat in your size," said the saleslady.

"This is my size," said Marigold. "And it's just the right color—purple! Next to my old coat, I love this better than any coat in the whole world."

"The sleeves are too short," said her mother.

"I can get purple mittens that come up to my elbows."

"It's too small," said her mother.

"I can get purple socks that come up over my knees."

"But the buttons won't even button," said her mother.

"I can get a purple scarf that comes down the front. And I'll get purple shoes and a purple hat, and big purple glasses. And I'll carry a purple purse and a purple umbrella. And everybody will say, 'Who's that?'"

Even so, Marigold still wore her old worn-out coat to bed.

After all, she was a very loyal person.

MARIGOLD'S NEW HOBBY

Marigold's last hobby had been inventing ugly faces,
and the hobby before that had been letting her hair grow.

Now she had a new hobby: making lists of things.

This is Marigold's first list:

Boring Things
- Taking turns
- Going to BED
- Shopping 4 coats!

Here is her second list:

Favorite Foods
* Popcorn sandwiches
* chocoLATE-covered CHOCOLATE
* CANDY SOUP!!
YUM YUM ← candy

This is another:

THINGS I will NEVER EAT
- JeLLYFiSH Soup
- WORM JuiCE EWW!!
- Fried PiMPLES
GROSS!

And another:

My Friends
1. OLD coat
2. Maxine

When Maxine came over, there was only one thing she wanted to know. "Why didn't you put me first?" she asked.

"Because my old coat is my best friend," said Marigold. "You're my next best."

"If I can't be first, then I don't want to be on the list at all," said Maxine.

"All right," said Marigold. And she crossed Maxine off.

"Now you don't have one single friend in the whole world," said Maxine.

"You don't have one single real friend." Then she went home.

"If I had too many friends, I wouldn't have enough time for my hobbies," Marigold said to her old coat.

She made a new list:

Her next list was:

And her next was:

Then she thought about how she could bug Maxine.

"I'm going to have a lemonade stand today," said Maxine as she walked past Marigold.

"Lemonade stands are boring," said Marigold. "The lemonade is always too sour or too sweet."

She thought for a minute. "I'm going to have a Special Surprise Treasure Stand. I'll have lots of packages, and no one will know what's inside until they open one."

"That's stupid," said Maxine. "Who wants to buy something when they don't know what it is?"

"Who wants to buy lemonade when they don't know whether it's too sweet or too sour?" asked Marigold. Then she went home and made a big sign.

Marigold gathered all the surprises and wrapped them up in pretty boxes.

She put the sign out in the front yard and waited for customers.

Before long, Maxine came back over.

"I thought you were having a lemonade stand," said Marigold.

"I'm done already," said Maxine. "I sold four paper cups of lemonade and made twenty cents."

Maxine looked at all the packages. "What's in this pink one?" she asked.

"That's for me to know and you to find out," said Marigold.

Maxine scratched her head. Then she reached into her pocket for one of her nickels. "I'll take it," she said.

Marigold gave Maxine the pink package. Maxine opened it.

"It's just a bunch of dirt!" she cried.

"It's not *just* a bunch of dirt," said Marigold. "There are worms in there, too."

"That's not a surprise package," said Maxine.

"Yes, it is," said Marigold. "You were surprised, weren't you?"

Marigold pointed
to the other packages,
then looked at Maxine.

"None of these has
dirt and worms inside,"
she said.

Maxine thought about
it. "I'll take the red one,"
she said finally.

Inside, she found three paper clips, two
thumbtacks, and one broken crayon.

"I'm not buying one more box," said Maxine. And she started to walk home.
"Now you'll never know what's in the rest of them," called Marigold.
Maxine stopped. She looked over her shoulder.

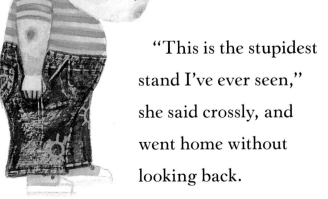

Then she walked back to the table. She bought the one wrapped in silver paper, which turned out to be filled with grass,

and with her last nickel she bought the one wrapped in polka-dot paper, which was filled with old chewing-gum wrappers and one piece of chewed gum.

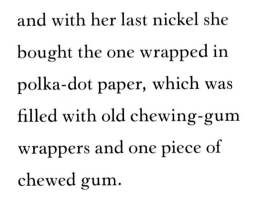

"This is the stupidest stand I've ever seen," she said crossly, and went home without looking back.

Marigold smiled.

"I guess I figured out how to bug her," she said to herself.

Tomorrow was the first day of school, and Marigold had nothing to wear. She wanted a fancy dress just like the one her favorite rock star wore, but her mother had said no.

"You have a closet filled with lovely clothes," her mother said.

Marigold hated every single thing that was in her closet. She thought her mother was unreasonable and stubborn, which was just what Marigold's mother thought about Marigold.

The next morning, Marigold sat on the front steps wearing her old coat and an orange cap that came down over her ears.

When Maxine came by, she said, "Look at my new plaid skirt. And look at my new tan jacket, and my new knee socks that match."

"I'm wearing a new red dress with sequins and sparkles under my coat," said Marigold.

But she wouldn't take off her coat.

"Look at my new gold locket," said Maxine.

"I'm wearing a new rhinestone necklace under my coat," said Marigold.

But she wouldn't take off her coat.

"My mother curled my hair this morning,"
said Maxine, tossing her curls.

"I dyed my hair purple and I have a new
spike haircut," said Marigold.
But she would not take off her cap.

Maxine looked at Marigold, and then she looked at her new plaid skirt and her nice new knee socks. She looked at Marigold again. "I'll be right back," she said. "I forgot something at home."

When Maxine came back, she was wearing a raincoat
and a green cap that came down over her ears.

"I decided to wear my new gold dress with sequins
and sparkles," she said.

But she wouldn't take off her raincoat.

"And I cut my hair and dyed it green."

But she would not take off her cap.

Marigold looked at Maxine. "I'm wearing rhinestone
bracelets that come up to my elbows," said Marigold.

"Me too," said Maxine.

Then Marigold and Maxine walked to school together in their coats and their caps that came down over their ears.

With much love to my wonderful children and their wonderful families—F.P.H.

For Robyn R.—my first best friend—with whom I set sail and navigated a stormy little friendship—J.M.

Published by Schwartz & Wade Books, an imprint of Random House Children's Books, a division of Random House, Inc., New York.

Text copyright © 2009 by Florence Parry Heide
Illustrations copyright © 2009 by Jill McElmurry

Schwartz & Wade Books and colophon are trademarks of Random House, Inc.

Visit us on the Web! www.randomhouse.com/kids
Educators and librarians, for a variety of teaching tools, visit us at www.randomhouse.com/teachers

Library of Congress Cataloging-in-Publication Data
Heide, Florence Parry.
The one and only Marigold / Florence Parry Heide ; illustrated by Jill McElmurry. — 1st ed.
p. cm.
Summary: Relates the misadventures of Marigold, who does not agree with anyone, as she shops with her mother for a coat, becomes interested in a new hobby, finds a way to "bug" her best friend, Maxine, and imaginatively copes with finding the right outfit for the first day of school.
ISBN 978-0-375-84031-9 (trade) — ISBN 978-0-375-94051-4 (lib. bdg.)
[1. Individuality—Fiction. 2. Family life—Fiction. 3. Friendship—Fiction.]
I. McElmurry, Jill, ill. II. Title.

PZ7.H36Mar 2009
[E]—dc22
2007037840

The text of this book is set in Horley Old Style.
The illustrations are rendered in gouache.
Book design by Rachael Cole

PRINTED IN MALAYSIA
1 2 3 4 5 6 7 8 9 10
First Edition